THE BUBBLE GUM CONTEST

Story by Michèle Dufresne
Illustrations by Tatjana Mai-Wyss

Contents

PIONEER VALLEY EDUCATIONAL PRESS, INC.

CHAPTER 1
THE POSTER

Spaceboy stood in front of a poster tacked to the notice board outside the post office. "Galaxy Girl, come look at this!" he called.

Galaxy Girl jumped off her scooter and joined Spaceboy in front of the notice board.

"Are you thinking of signing up?" asked Galaxy Girl. "It sounds like fun! You're great at blowing bubbles. I bet you'd win!"

"Yeah," said Spaceboy. "But I already have a scooter. I'm thinking of Space Monster."

"Space Monster!" said Galaxy Girl. "But, he is very shy. Plus, I'm not sure he knows how to blow bubbles."

"We can teach him!" said Spaceboy. "You know how much he wants a flying scooter like ours!"

Bubble Gum Blowing
Contest

sponsored by : The Asteroid Bubble
Gum Company

Time : July 15 11 :30

Location : The Community Theater

First Prize : A green and
white flying scooter

5

CHAPTER 2
PRACTICE

At first Space Monster refused to sign up for the contest. He really, really wanted the flying scooter, but he was very shy and frightened of getting up on stage in front of a lot of people.

Finally, Spaceboy and Galaxy Girl convinced Space Monster he could do it.

So the bubble lessons began.

They went to the store and bought an
extra large box of
Asteroid Bubble Gum.

Spaceboy showed Space Monster how to
hold the gum in his hand to warm
it up, then, how to chew it until it was
just the right consistency.
Next, Space Monster learned how to
control his breath and blow and blow.

After days of practicing,
Galaxy Girl said, "You know something,
Space Monster, you are good at this.
You could win!"

One day they were practicing in the park. They made Space Monster stand on a park bench. He was pretending to be on stage.

"Ready, set, go!" called Spaceboy.

Space Monster blew and blew. Soon he had a huge bubble. The bubble was almost the size of Space Monster's face.

Spaceboy was going to measure
the bubble when suddenly
Space Monster took a breath and the
bubble broke and gum covered
Space Monster's face.

Space Monster sat down on the bench.
"I can't do this," he said.
He tried to wipe away the gum.

"You can do it," said Galaxy Girl.
She began to wipe at the bubble gum
stuck to Space Monster's face.

Space Monster
thought about
the first prize,
the green and
white scooter.
He really, really
wanted that flying scooter.

"OK," he said.
"Let's practice some more."

CHAPTER 3
THE CONTEST

The morning of the contest
was warm and sunny. Everyone
gathered at Spaceboy's house.
Spaceboy's mother made pancakes
and bacon for breakfast.

After everyone had eaten,
Spaceboy said, "I think Space Monster
should practice some more.
We have a few more hours
before the contest starts."

"Maybe Space Monster should rest,"
said Galaxy Girl.

"Hmm," said Spaceboy.
"Maybe you're right. Then he will have
lots of air for the contest."

They all lay down on the floor to rest,
but Spacedog kept jumping on them.
Finally they gave up and played a game
of Space Race while they waited for the
contest to begin.

Finally it was time for the contest. The twelve contestants lined up on the stage at the community theater. Spaceboy and Galaxy Girl knew this was the hardest part for Space Monster, who was very shy. They could see Space Monster at the end of the line of contestants rolling his piece of gum around in his hand, warming it up like they had taught him.

Pluto Boy, also in the contest, was tossing his gum from hand to hand and grinning.

"Ready, set, go," said the Asteroid Bubble Gum representative.

The twelve contestants popped their gum into their mouths and began to chew. Soon almost everyone was blowing, but not Space Monster. He kept chewing until the gum was just right for blowing.

Soon you could hear **pop, pop, pop,** as one by one, the contestants' bubbles popped.

Then it was just Pluto Boy and Space Monster left blowing.
Pluto Boy's face was turning from orange to purple.

Space Monster was taking deep, even breaths. All of his antennae were waving wildly while he blew.

Then pop! Pluto Boy's bubble popped. There was bubble gum all over his face!

Space Monster kept blowing.
The bubble got bigger and bigger
until it was as big as his whole face.
The crowd went wild. It was the biggest
bubble anyone had ever seen.

"And we have a winner!" cried the
Asteroid Bubble Gum Representative.
"Space Monster!"

"Hooray! Hooray!" cried Galaxy Girl
and Spaceboy. "You did it, Space
Monster! You did it!"